What Not To Give Your Mom On Mother's Day

by **Martha Simpson**

illustrated by **Jana Christy**

Amazon Children's Publishing

Text copyright © 2013 by Martha Simpson
Illustrations copyright © 2013 by Jana Christy

All rights reserved
Amazon Publishing
Attn: Amazon Children's Publishing
P.O. Box 400818
Las Vegas, NV 89140
www.amazon.com/amazonchildrenspublishing

Library of Congress Cataloging-in-Publication Data
is available upon request
ISBN-13: 9781477816479 (hardcover)
ISBN-10: 147781647X (hardcover)
ISBN-13 9781477866474 (eBook)
ISBN-10: 1477866477 (eBook)

The illustrations are rendered digitally.
Book design by Vera Soki
Editor: Margery Cuyler

Printed in China (R)
First edition, 2013
10 9 8 7 6 5 4 3 2 1

To Paul, Rose, Nick, and Shayna—with love from Mom—M.S.

For my mom, Betty. I love you, Ma.—J.C.

MOTHER'S DAY is coming soon.
What should you give your mom?
Well, it depends.

But here is my advice on
what **NOT** to give her.

Do **NOT** give her a bucket of big, fat worms. . .

unless she is a bird.

"Tweet, tweet! Plump, juicy worms!"

Do **NOT** give her a beat-up shoe...

unless she is a dog.

Do **NOT** give her dead flies. . .

unless she is a salamander.

"Slip,
slide!
Just right for laying my eggs!"

Do NOT give her a block of salt . . .

Do **NOT** give her a pile of sticks. . .

unless she is a beaver.

"Slap, slap! Sticks to build my dam!"

Do NOT give her a mound of termites...

unless she is an aardvark.

Do **NOT** give her a mud puddle. . .

unless she is a pig.

"Oink, oink! This really cools me off!"

Do NOT give her some mosquitoes...

unless she is a bat.

"Squee, squee! I'll eat those pesky skeeters!"

But there is something you could give your mother...

a big hug and a kiss! I love you, too, honey!